Just a Passing Phrase II

Mary Easty

Collated by Richard Easty

Contents

Annie Says

Annie's nephew is getting a bit cheeky — she hopes it's just a passing phrase.

A Good Day Out

"Have you got any plans for today?" Eric asked.

Pat was glad he was washing up and didn't notice her blushing.

"Not really? Why?"

"Do you mind if I take the car?" he said, "I'll have to go to the club again this morning. The competition starts very soon and there's a lot of new players out there. One or two of them are really good." He sighed and smiled. "I've got to practice."

"Oh, that's alright," she said quickly, "I thought I might call on Jan again, she didn't look well the other day. I can manage with the old banger, it's perfectly safe on the side roads. What time would you like to eat?"

"Sixish OK?" he checked. "Fine, I'll be back before then," she agreed.

Eric wiped his hands and hurried upstairs to get ready, soon down again in his new outfit. Nice jumper, thought Pat, but the bright patterned trousers were a bit... well... bright, some of the clothes he'd bought recently. She smiled at the jaunty yellow cap as he grabbed his bag and raced off, shouting "Have a good day!" "And you!" she called.

As soon as the car pulled away, she picked up the phone, dialled, listened as it rang 3 times, then put it down quickly, and ran upstairs herself. A quick shower, a hasty riffle through the wardrobe, a careful check in the mirror, and she too was ready to leave, turning not towards the motorway like Eric but out of town on the quieter routes.

About five o'clock, Pat was driving back towards home, her expression decidedly glum. "What a fool," she was saying to herself. "Can't think I could have believed all that nonsense.

What a fool". Tears ran down her face till she could hardly see the road ahead. She did, however, notice the fuel gauge... almost empty.

"What else can go wrong?" she wept, then gritting her teeth and sniffling she swerved and changed direction, nearly causing the driver behind to run into her, and aimed for the motorway. The nearest petrol station was full of cars "as of course it would be" she grumbled and she had to pull over near some bushes to wait. She blew her nose and wiped her eyes and looked round and suddenly saw the jaunty golfing cap, Eric filling up the tank of their car. Pat sat still, not to be seen, as he went into the office to pay, then her gaze turned idly to the car. "What!" she thought. There was a very pretty young woman in the passenger-seat!

Slowly and carefully Pat retrieved the bird-watching binoculars from the glove compartment and focussed them. My word, she thought, that woman looks angry. Very angry, actually. Thin, taut lips, fierce eyes, cheeks red with fury.

Eric returned to the car and Pat crouched lower, eyes fixed on the passenger, who ignored him, just gazed straight ahead. The car slowly passed her hiding place, and she could see Eric's embarrassed and disappointed expression. Even the cap didn't look jaunty any more.

In deep thought, Pat got some petrol. Then on her way home she bought two good steaks and some strawberries and cream. When she reached home she started to prepare the evening meal.

Eric arrived quite soon. He walked in, threw his clubs into the corner of the hall and his cap after them. He sat on the stairs and flung off his shoes, and sat there for a bit, thinking.

Some time later, whilst they were setting the table, Pat

asked casually, "Well, what did you get up to today?" "Nothing actually," he answered. "I can't handle the competition these days, too many young people around now." He sighed. Then, "How was your day?" "Waste of time," she said, "I shan't go again, I'm not wanted there any more." They sat in silence.

"There's a nice smell," Eric said after a bit. "Oh! I almost let it burn!" Pat leapt up and rescued the dinner. As they ate, Eric asked "Have you any plans for tomorrow, then?"

"No, not really," said Pat, unfortunately blushing a little, but as usual he didn't notice. Then he said, "Well, neither have I. Let's decide where we'd like to go. We could have a nice day out!" and he dropped another dollop of cream onto his strawberries.

Annie Says

Annie loves flying but she doesn't like the taking off or landing, so she sympathises with Mr. Prescott when he says he's always glad to get back on terra cotta.

Traffic Report

On the main road there is a crossing place, with stripes, buttons, and a green man. It provides a safe passage for the staff of the nearby hospital, the patients and their visitors. It also provides a link between the little parade of shops on one side and the Post Office on the other.

People living in the area use the crossing all the time, and it is particularly useful for two great friends, both well over ninety, who go out each morning to buy their day's provisions. They are very small, both under five feet tall — petite when they were young, but even tinier as time has bent their backs and stooped their knees. One is Miss S, former formidable senior teacher at the local high school.

There had been no larking about in Miss S's classes, no loud voices or scuffles. One sharp glance would reduce six-foot adolescents to shambling apologies, desperate to avoid her gargoyle gaze.

Her neighbour is Mrs D, widow of the dreaded (though long departed) dentist, known in his day as the Driller, to whose surgery unwilling patients were summoned for probing checks and painful treatment. Mrs D had been the dragon at the end of his telephone, meticulously examining the unlikely excuses for non-attendance and making firm appointments for repeats.

These two neighbours would meet each day at their garden gates, armed with their trolleys, and make their way to the crossing. One morning they changed their routine slightly, only very slightly, but it had an unexpected effect. Mrs D had a rather sore heel, so they decided that she would not cross the road but would wait by the lights as Miss S picked up their shopping and brought it back to be shared appropriately, and then they would trundle their trolleys back for a cup of tea at Mrs D's flat. So it was that Miss S appeared at the shop doorway with her load, Mrs D pressed the button, and the people at each side watched for the green man.

The lights changed, the signal bleeped, the people grouped and set out. Just behind Mrs D were two builders who had almost finished putting up a new garage behind the post office. They were keenly anticipating the steak pies available, hot, from the butcher, and were wishing that Mrs D would hurry up before the green man disappeared. When it became clear that she was not about to step off the pavement, the hungry young men grinned at each other, and with words of cheery encouragement, "Come on, love," they took her arms and started to propel her across. Of course she tried to resist, but she was so much smaller and lighter than they were that they had no idea that she was so reluctant.

The groups approached each other like the two lines in a country dance. In the centre of one group was Miss S, head down, heaving the heavy trolley. Halfway across the road she heard the furious squeals of her friend's voice, and looked up in astonishment as Mrs D almost passed her, crimson-faced, hat askew, shoes kicking in the air. The trolleys met and locked, and like synchronised swimmers the two friends sank gently, gracefully and very softly beneath the waves, landing quite lightly and unhurt, amongst the legs of the crowd now milling around them.

Consternation reigned. "There's two old women had an accident!" Mrs D heard someone shout, which added to her rage. What an indelicate phrase! "Ladies", surely, "Elderly" perhaps, but "Accident!" certainly not! She tried to get to her feet, as a figure pushed its way towards her.

"I'm a nurse," someone announced. People stood back respectfully. One of the builders, conscience pricking, offered to carry Miss S and Mrs D to the safety of the pavement, but was abruptly rebuffed. "You should never move a casualty" he was told, "there may be broken bones and any injuries could be made worse." The nurse unbuttoned her coat and revealed a watch, swinging on her ample uniform. "Injuries! Rubbish!" Miss S hissed, her voice muffled by the noise around her. "Just let us get up ..."

Shopkeepers were appearing now with blankets and the two victims were rolled up like Egyptian mummies. Solicitous bystanders took off their coats and put them under the ladies' heads. Compassionate hands patted them and excited faces closed in on them mouthing "You'll be all right, love, don't worry, just try to keep calm." A bus, unable to get past the crammed crossing, backed up so the passengers could have a better view. A man jumped off and introduced himself as a traffic warden (boos) on his way to work (more boos) and pledged himself to sort out the traffic (ironic applause). He importantly held up some cars which had already stopped, and made the drivers get out and lend their Triangles, which he then set out in a Special Pattern in the road. No vehicles could move in any case, and traffic was in a solid mass as far as the motorway.

Several people had called for the police on their mobiles, and three cars arrived at the same time. The officers got out and had a conference at the side of the road, glancing across towards Miss S and Mrs D, who were submerged entirely by the mob around them, still protesting unheard and unheeded. The policemen set up a board saying "Accident, can-U-help," and called through a loud hailer for witnesses.

An extraordinary number of people joined the queue to tell the police their theories about the incident. Two reporters from the local paper recorded all these statements and rushed back to their office.

Three or four young women clutching clipboards tunnelled their way into the chaos, asking everyone whose attention they could catch, "Have you had an accident recently? Was it your fault?" People racked their brains but few could come up with the correct answer, and the solicitors' runners ran about more frantically, able to sniff their quarry but not hunt them down. "No win, no fee!" they encouraged, but their desperate cries were unsuccessful.

The nurse was still trying to find Mrs D's pulse when there was a moment's silence. A huge car drew up, and a loud voice was heard, asking what had happened. "I'll have a look" was the decision. "You a Doc, mate?" somebody asked. "A Consultant," was the reply. A large man of about 50 years approached, and a path appeared as the impressed crowd shuffled out of his way. Handing his well-cut silk jacket for the rather miffed nurse to hold he flicked up his shirt sleeves, revealing gold bracelets and an expensive watch. The crowd drew in its collective breath in appreciation as he ran his hands down what bits of Mrs D he could actually touch outside the swaddling bonds. He nodded wisely.

Two young men who had followed him down the path and had reached the epicentre of the incident at the same time, watched him in some amusement. "Pretty amateurish examination," one commented. "Obstetrician, what did you expect?" replied the other, both speaking just loudly enough for the consultant to overhear. He rose hurriedly, dusted off his trousers and snatched up his jacket. "Morning, doctors," he said, turning to his car. "Morning, Sir," they chorused. "Leave the patients where they are," he instructed as he retreated. The nurse looked pleased, but the two younger men took no notice, checked our friends with practised hands, reassured them and began to help them up, just as two ambulances arrived, one from each direction. The crowd drew in again. "Here's the Paramedics," came the glad cry from the onlookers, who had started to look really disappointed when it had seemed the show was nearly over.

Large men approached, staggering under the weight of stretchers, heart monitors, yet more (but Official Red) blankets, and excitement began to build up again as the sirens shrieked dissonantly. Miss S and Mrs D exchanged meaningful looks. They had no intention of being swept off anywhere.

Suddenly the most exhilarating contribution of all occurred - the Police helicopter could be heard in the distance, homing in on the Incident. The delighted crowds, by now several hundred deep, craned upwards to watch the elegant machine circle closely above them. Many people waved, some even cheered, but not too loudly out of respect for whatever had caused this bit of theatre. As everyone strained on tiptoe, Miss S and Mrs D crawled to the pavement, dragging their trolleys along the stripes, and made their getaway.

Shortly afterwards they sat on Mrs D's balcony with a cup of tea and watched the crowds drift off. The heroic medics and other officials returned to work with excellent excuses for late arrival. Those who had so much enjoyed the morning went home to regale their families with fairly inaccurate and exaggerated details, that no one believed.

The day wore on, and Miss S looked round for her jacket,

but Mrs D noticed something else happening across the road, and put two eggs on to boil.

Outside her flower-shop, Mrs P was filling buckets with hastily-tied bunches of coloured daises. Her daughter Polly propped one up against a wall by the green man. The flowers soon caught the eye of passers-by and before long the shop was filled with eager customers.

Ranks of bouquets wrapped in stiff paper took up most of the pavement, many of them bedecked with messages. Mrs D called down to the paper boy and asked him what they said. "In memory of a dear friend" was one he read solemnly. "You will never be forgotten" was another.

Miss S turned to Mrs D.

"You don't think we should — ?" Her voice trailed away.

"Certainly not!" said Mrs D briskly. "It would only add to the confusion".

Their eyes met, and they began to laugh. As they dabbed their eyes, Mrs D offered "Have another slice of Victoria sponge".

As Miss S let herself out of the front gate, young girls were arranging shining candles amongst the tributes. Mr J. at the Post Office almost ran out of stock. Mothers smiled proudly as small children on their way home from school gave little teddy bears, though some of them had to be dragged away, reluctant to leave them behind.

The two builders, whose kindly-meant intervention had started it all off, began to see the funny side in the pub that night, but could never tell anyone what had happened in case they were charged with causing a riot.

Heavy overnight rain battered the bouquets against the pavement. The wrapping paper fell off and swirled down the flooded gutters, decorated with flower heads and cards. Delighted children on their way to school tugged on their mothers' hands and leaned over the puddles to snatch little toys from the mud.

A lollipop lady patrolled the crossing, slowly and majestically, to the annoyance of drivers who found that the green man was not always in sync with her forays, and swerved as near as they dared to the deepest pools. Soaked shoppers complained and the lollipop lady was called off at lunchtime.

After the rush hour, a council van was despatched to clear up the rubbish still choking the drains, and after a while a police car removed the "danger" signs and put up others which begged for witnesses to a "serious accident" which had occurred in this area. Several people helpfully made a note of the email address though in many cases they didn't have a computer. Before long, some of the boards blew away down the road.

It was "pension day" and Mrs D and Miss S had to go to the post office in spite of the dreadful weather. There was the usual grumbling queue round the counters and even some hardy souls crouching under umbrellas on the steps. Mr J smiled down at them through the grille. "Don't suppose you saw much of yesterday's accident?" he inquired." "No, too many people around us," Mrs. D. replied as she walked out again into the storm.

The local newspaper came out rather late that week, with the headline on page two: "Not many Injured," and carried a slightly blurred photograph of the helicopter. The front page led with a large picture of the opening of the new garage behind the Post Office. The title was "Builders make Impact in our Area."

Incident at Coniston

Our friend George is a keen walker. Long ago, when he was a teenager working in the city, he was taken to the Lake District by the local Boys' Club, and never forgot the beauty and the challenge that he found there. This started a lifelong enthusiasm for the hills. Later he joined a mountaineering club where he learnt from the professional guide Jim Ryder how to climb safely. Some of his proudest and most cherished memories are of the times he was called out with the volunteers of the Mountain Rescue Team when Jim was the leader, and helped to bring people down to safety.

Now George has retired he is up in the Lakes every week with his companions, and as they retrace their favourite routes and discover new ones their conversation often turns to adventures they have shared. They all remember Jim and speak of him with the greatest admiration and respect.

At the end of last summer, a young nephew from Canada came to stay with George and his wife. He was a fit, strong, sports-mad teenager, longing to go out with George for a day. Thinking of himself at that age, George chose a suitable route, checked the weather forecast, made sure that Keith was properly dressed and equipped, and they set off early.

The morning went well. The day was clear and the views were wonderful, the paths high but not too steep. They ate their lunch at a sheltered spot, but, as they packed up afterwards, Keith stepped back to swing his rucksack onto his shoulder, put his foot onto a loose rock, and fell awkwardly. Looking at the swelling ankle, George knew that the boy would not be able to walk any further.

George's first thought was "What would Jim do?" Then

he shook himself and smiled. This was up to him. He made Keith as comfortable as possible, well wrapped up in a survival bag with his rucksack close by containing their remaining food and extra clothes, and explained that he would go down on his own to fetch help. Keith had the torch and whistle, and waved George off bravely.

George walked down steadily, knowing it would be at least two hours before he reached the Mountain Rescue Post, and the same back to reach Keith. In his mind he went over and over the precautions he had taken for Keith's safety, and felt the unseen support of his old friend.

The light was going when he reached the Rescue Post and explained to the member on call what had happened. He felt a rush of emotion as the team began to assemble, called in as he had been so long ago. Relief flooded over him as the responsibility for getting help was lifted from his shoulders, yet he still knew the episode was not over. He asked the new leader for news of Jim.

"Jim?" said the young man. "Did you know him?" George nodded. "Sorry to tell you - he died a year or two ago. Up on the tops, of course, walking his dogs, as he would have wanted. Getting on, you know, hadn't been on the Rescue for years by then, but you couldn't keep him off the hills!"

George walked back with the team, the younger faster men making much better time and carrying him along with them. Keith was there, flashing his torch and shouting as they got nearer, apologising for needing them. They were bluff, friendly, businesslike, helping George too, who by now was quite exhausted.

"You've done well," they said to Keith. "Nasty up here for you in the dark, waiting for us."

"Not really," said Keith. "A friend of George's came by with his dogs, and he kept me company for a bit. He's not been gone long."

The volunteers glanced at each other and at George, and looked away quickly. Pulling up their collars against the invading chill they shouldered the stretcher and turned down towards the distant lights.

Annie Says

Young people are so impatient, Annie says. They should remember Rome wasn't burnt in a day.

The Rain Came Down In Torrents

The rain was coming down in torrents, huge drops hammering on the window panes, drumming on the roof of the cottage. Heavy gusts of wind howled against the stone walls and shrieked through the gaps round the doorway.

She crouched under her duvet, eyes staring at the patched ceiling, hoping not to notice any wet patches She thought of the poem she had learnt at school - "This house has been far out at sea all night," - and understood what Ted Hughes meant.

The cottage was old and in poor repair. She had been warned when she first planned to move in, but had so loved her childhood holidays there; of course in those days Grannie had been in charge, knowing where to arrange buckets and mop up the puddles and laugh at the problems in her little house.

The main worry now was whether He would be able to get through to her next morning, as had been promised. Without him, how could she survive? The cottage was to be a secret hideaway, where she could write, walk, watch the birds, but all her plans depended on him. Without him, she thought again, how could she cope?

Looking at the map she had followed from the motorway, she ran her finger along the A roads, then the B roads, then the winding lanes, retracing the route in her mind.

The final narrow turn, and the ford! oh! She caught her breath - that would be deep and deepening now, the way so narrow, the trees so enveloping, the wood so dark. What if he gave up and turned back? He wouldn't have the mobile number here, nor she his, and anyway the cottage was so far from everywhere there probably would be no signal.

As daylight began to break through above the canopy of old trees, the heavy downpour relented a little and the wind eased. A steady trickle, like thick mist clouded the cottage windows. She washed, dressed, made a cup of tea, watched.

The lane was a little clearer from her bedroom window, so she went back upstairs and pulled up a chair. She tried to write, but her imagination had dried up, even if the rain had not. How far would he have got by now? she worried. What time would he have set out? This whole adventure depended on him. As the clock ticked on she wondered if she would have to pack up and go home, a failure, to brave the knowing "told you so."

The morning was passing slowly, the room warmed up and she dozed uneasily in her easy chair, wakening at every sound.

Suddenly, she shot to her feet, scrubbing at the misted glass - surely she could hear an engine! Full of hope she raced unsteadily down the stairs, leapt the last few steps, flung open the door - and joy! There he was! She was so relieved, thankful, rushed down the slippery path and through the soaking plants and hugged the man heaving himself out of his van. "I thought you might not get here," she sobbed.

"You shouldn't have worried!" he said, disentangling himself from her arms and opening the doors of the van.

"Tesco's drivers always get through!"

November

We are walking slowly up a steep hill.   The ground is muddy, and we squelch and stumble. The path winds and the views change, and as we get higher we can make out other paths along the nearby hillsides. We see people, dressed like us in thick fleeces and warm cagoules and heavy boots, heads down against the wind, glad the rain is holding off.

The routes converge near the top of our hill, the highest, and we are reaching outcrops of rock exposed by centuries of bleak weather. The going is quite difficult now and everyone is quiet, concentrating on keeping our balance.

Round the last bend we see the stark outline of the cenotaph, our reason for gathering here today. We push between the huge stones and on to sparse grass, breathing hard.

We watch the others making their way from other directions, and are reminded of those who came secretly to hear John Wesley, or other preachers who were forbidden to give their message years ago. We are all short of breath! And the only sound is of shuffling boots and the shrieking wind.

The minister stands in the lee of the cenotaph, his robes buffeted round his legs, and we wonder if he will take off over the distant reservoirs. The brave Youth Band, brass instruments polished to glisten in the bursts of sunshine, start the service as wreaths are placed. The territorials, the cadets, the Legion, the mayor, solemnly step forward in turn, and weigh down their flowers as the blasts of wind carry our voices away. "Oh God, our help in ages past" we sing stoutly. The minister leads the short service, and then announces the Two Minute Silence.

We stand our ground. Sometimes a dog barks, down below

us, but we are all lost in our own thoughts. We look at the poppies, we look across these familiar, bare but beautiful hills, the silence so encompassing that we are far away.

Suddenly, the hooters of all the mills around Oldham startle us, jerk us back into the moment. We cough, and shuffle our feet, and look at each other again. We unpin our own poppies and place them on the steps by the names of men and women we never knew.

Then, back to life, we retrace our steps and leave Pots and Pans for another year.

Annie Says

Annie was not impressed by a woman on TV. She never said anything, she just sat there grinning like a Cheshire Cheese.

The Valentine

Eleanor had always loved Monday mornings since her first day at Fisher's. She looked forward to Mondays as the other girls in the office looked forward to Fridays, and every weekend she washed her newest blouse, pressed her skirt, and set her hair, so that when the day came she could start out for work confident of looking her best.

This morning she checked her reflection in the bus window, her eyes darkening as her mind turned back to that first Monday at Fisher's. Straight from school, Eleanor had been taken into the main office which had seemed huge, full of other girls watching her. Standing uncomfortably by the Chief Clerk, Miss Williams, she had tried to take in all the instructions — then the door had burst open and everyone had turned to stare at the crimson young man who stood there open-mouthed in surprise and embarrassment at the giggling girls.

Mr Fisher had come out of his office. "I — I was sent here..." Frank had stammered. Mr Fisher and even Miss Williams had smiled. Apparently this was the joke played on all the new apprentices: the other men had sent him on some errand telling him to force the door open — a trick which worked every time! Mr Fisher rescued Frank with some considerate phrase, and had added, "We have somebody new in our office today, too, Frank," indicating Eleanor, who in turn blushingly shuffled her feet.

Eleanor smiled now, looking back, for that had been the Beginning of Everything. Every week over the years since that fateful Monday, Frank brought Mr Fisher the invoices from his department, and always paused at her desk for a special chat.

"Here's your boy-friend, Eleanor!" the other girls teased,

and it still continued, even though the girls had changed, some leaving to be married or have children, and Eleanor herself was now the Chief Clerk. Frank too had a senior position now in his office, but he still delivered the invoices himself, and Eleanor thought she knew the reason why.

Today, however, was going to be even more special than the usual Mondays, for Eleanor had a plan to carry out. This was not just any Monday, it was also Valentine's Day. Over the years, February 14th had always had an effect in the office — for days before, the girls had brought in the cards they had chosen to send. "Have you bought yours yet, Eleanor?" they would ask, and she would say lightly, "Some of them!" though she had never actually done so, for who would she have given one to?

Then on the Day, the girls would arrive laughing and pleased with the cards they had received, passing them round with gasps and giggles, sometimes coy, sometimes cheeky, and again, "Did you get some Valentines, Eleanor?" and she would reply "You know me!" in a mysterious voice — though the postman would have brought bills or a letter from her sister if he had called at all.

This year, however, Eleanor had resolved, would be different. After all this time, surely Frank would make a move, and if he daren't then perhaps it was up to her. She thought a Valentine might be a "jokey" way of letting him see she was — just a bit — "interested". Unfortunately, looking round the shelves in the newsagent's shop, Eleanor felt that the cards seemed very outspoken, some she considered quite crude, and certainly not suitable for her purpose. In the end she had settled on a large one from a rack labelled "Open: for your own message" and picked out a flowery picture with a couple of hearts entwined on a satin cushion. When she came to write her "own message", though, she couldn't think what to put, and so far the card was blank.

As the bus turned into Church Street, Eleanor opened her bag and checked that she had the card with her. She took it out of its wrapper and put it on top of all her other things, so that when a suitable message occurred to her she would be able to write it in quickly before handing it to Frank, which she hoped could be accomplished discreetly without all the girls noticing. However — and here she smiled again to herself — there was always the hope that he might be carrying a card himself...

As usual on February 14th the office was high with excitement and laughter, and as Eleanor hurried through to the washroom to hang up her coat and check her appearance the girls were shrieking as they compared their Valentines. Mr Fisher arrived and things quietened down a bit, just the odd snorts and sniggers as a new card was passed round. Then the door opened and in came Frank. Eleanor couldn't help blushing as their eyes met, and she could see the girls noticed his nod and smile. Frank went first to Mr Fisher, and Eleanor suddenly remembered she hadn't written her message yet. She fumbled in her bag, and looked up to see Frank already by her desk, looking, she realised, rather flustered.

"Eleanor," he said quietly, leaning towards her, "I've got something for you. I don't want the others to know yet." Eleanor saw he had an envelope in his hand and her heart thudded. Surely... "We've known each other for a long time," Frank was saying, "and I've meant to tell you this before..." He was very close now, holding out the envelope. "I want you to be the first to know," he said, "I'm getting married next month!

I've brought you an invitation."

Eleanor couldn't believe what she was hearing. The other girls, obviously trying to work out what was happening, were watching them closely.

She glanced down and realised she was holding two envelopes now, the one Frank had given her and the one she had intended for him. Suddenly she knew what to do. "What exciting news!" she said loudly, giving him a hearty kiss on the cheek. "But you didn't fool me! I guessed all along really! Look, I've even brought a card for you in case you were going to announce it today!" and smiling broadly she wrote "To an old friend, wishing you every happiness, from Eleanor."

Annie Says

Annie's gardener wears toe-nailed boots for protection when he mows the lawn.

Sweet Charity

On a cold, wet and blustery day in early October I went into town on the bus. Shortly before we reached the city centre, we pulled in outside a busy Post Office, and as we waited for passengers to get on and off I looked through the window. It was "pension day", and the shop and the pavement outside were crowded, mainly with elderly people collecting their week's money and pausing to chat before going home, their cheerful faces and colourful umbrellas reflected in the puddles.

Amongst them was a young man, the collar of his thin jacket turned up against the rain, a metal ring or stud of some kind glinting on his face. Most of the older people seemed to know him, greeting him in a friendly manner and drawing him into their groups. As I became interested I saw he had a shiny box on a string round his neck, and I realised that many people were putting money into it. Each time, he thanked them, laughing and joking with them as if they were old friends, moving easily amongst them. As the driver put the bus into gear and we pulled away, I heard the Collector say to an old lady, "Needy children, love?" and another slow, trembling hand reached into a bag and took out a coin, being rewarded with a glowing smile and a touch on the arm.

Somehow I felt uncomfortable with this. It seemed as though the Collector was taking advantage of these people, who might not be able to afford the donations they were making, but did not like to refuse. "What a shame," I thought, "it's probably not even genuine! Looks as though he waits there every week for them." The bus moved on and I forgot about the scene.

After lunch I called in at the book shop, which was full

of new students buying their first text books. Mindful of the sacrifices being made at home to enable them to get to college, they were choosing their books carefully, taking the minimum for their courses and arranging to share others. As I emerged into the faltering sunlight amongst a little group, I heard the mantra again. "Needy children?" The same friendly smile, but not quite the same expression. Where previously the Collector had been everyone's favourite grandson, now he was "one of the gang." They couldn't resist him. He had his act off to perfection. Sly admiration for the girls, "Thanks, mate" for the young men, a satisfying chink of coins into the box.

I was delayed during the afternoon, and was walking towards the bus station through the office area as the City businessmen and women were making for their cars. The rain was lashing down once more and the light was rapidly dying away. I was hardly surprised to make out the figure of the Collector yet again, under the cover of the stone arcades around the Law Courts. I was interested to see how he would approach his new prey, so I stood to one side, arranging my parcels, to watch.

This time, he was almost an object of pity, no flashing smiles, no confident repartee - almost a whine - "Needy children, sir?" The well-dressed "victims" caught the suppressed shiver, the deferential glance, the grateful acknowledgement. More contributed than I would have expected, and then hurried on, no doubt feeling themselves fortunate to be leaving the cold and desolate city, and looking forward to a good meal.

As I approached the bus station I saw the Collector walking ahead along the same route, moving quickly now, purposefully. My interest was rekindled as I followed, wryly reflecting on his skill in handling the different groups of people he had met during the day. I estimated that he must have made quite a sum.

I turned into the yard and searched along the rows of buses for the one which would take me home. It had drawn in at the back of the rank, several minutes early, and I was the first person to board. It was still unlit, and I cleared a dry patch so I could look through the misty window. The first thing I saw was the Collector, leaning against a pillar, smoking a cigarette.

Suddenly my attention was caught by a movement in the shadows, and then another. I realised that, one by one, figures were creeping out from the concrete doorways, approaching the young man with the collecting-box. What was going on? Were they going to attack him? I watched intently as they reached him, and as I stared I began to recognise some of them - well-known frightening creatures from the city streets - the rolling drunk who usually lay in the gutter behind the Town Hall, the terrifying baglady who roars and swears her way up and down Deansgate with her mobile home in a broken supermarket trolley, the tiny teenage girl who sits on a blanket in King Street, staring down at her plastic bowl - all these and other familiars were gathering round the Collector.

As I watched, he opened his box and shared out the coins amongst them. There was no jostling, no pushing, no speech passed between them. Amazingly, he seemed to have assumed yet another personality, warm, gentle and comfortable, and I sensed the trust of these cold, hardened, sad outcasts, depending on the Collector for food and shelter. As the bus pulled out, I remembered his words: "Needy children, please."

A Country Life: Hetty

Hetty lived all her life close to the river Wye. As a child, she grew up on her father's smallholding at the edge of the Forest of Dean. Streams converging from the Welsh hills gathered together for the long journey north, providing the family with water for drinking and washing and tending the plot. On fine days, Hetty and her sisters would paddle, or have tea-parties with their wooden dolls. At times of heavy rain or melting snow, they splashed about in the swirling mud to rescue the ducks and hens.

When Hetty married, she moved downstream to her husband Tom's small farm below Ross. Here the river meandered in a huge circle about the town. Apples for cider were their main business, but in a field that stretched down to the water a few cows were kept, standing shoulder-deep on summer days to keep cool. Hetty's children played in the shallows, learning to swim and to manage their boat.

Hetty loved the river in all its moods. She knew it when, staid and serene, it hosted the local regattas, and the banks were covered with picnicking families, and red-faced oarsmen panted past, following the orders of the megaphoned coaches cycling along the towpath. She respected it when in the spring or autumn it grew fierce and dangerous, menacing the bridges and overflowing into the culverts, often so deep that the drains filled too and the surrounding land was covered.

When Tom died, in his eighties, and the children were far away with families of their own, Hetty left the farm and took a cottage nearby. She kept busy with housekeeping and a little shopping, and spent long hours sitting at her window watching the birds and boats and of course the river, passing at the end of her garden. Then one day she had a fall, and all kinds of things came to the attention of her friends and neighbours. They found that she had fallen once or twice before. What was more startling, they discovered Hetty was very nearly a hundred years old! It was decided she should move again ("for the time being," they promised her, "just until she was better") into a nursing home just outside Hereford.

She agreed to this plan only because the house they chose was called "River View", but unfortunately it stood on a lane across the wide water meadows, and the Wye could be seen only when the sun caught it, silver and glistening, in the distance. For the first time in her life Hetty could not see the water, nor could she hear its music. Like a clock whose ticking and striking suddenly stops, the river's silence disturbed her. Hetty did not improve as quickly as had been expected, and she spent more and more time in bed, sleeping for most of the day.

One October morning she wakened to the sound of gales lashing against her window. It had been raining hard for days, but now the wind was high, bending the trees in a mad dance, and tumbling the birds about the sky. The clouds were low and heavy, and the nurses came into work complaining about the gusts and shaking the water off their coats. Hetty, slowly wakening, believed herself to be a child again.

She saw her mother calling her in, smoothing down her apron as it flapped about her head. Hetty and her sisters struggled to close the door of the hen-house, and the water butts overflowed.

In the afternoon, the wind rose to a shriek, and along the corridors outside Hetty's room doors slammed and windows strained against the pressure. News was coming in of floods approaching the city, waves rolling in places over the river-banks. As Hetty drifted in and out of sleep she caught little snatches of excited chatter as the nurses worried about getting home. Now Hetty was a farmer's wife again, her husband Tom out in the field driving the cows up to higher ground. For a moment she was holding the heavy door open, lamp held high, as he came in from the storm.

The wind settled later and the early evening was quieter. Hetty was more alert when the suppers were brought round. As the nurses propped her up amongst her pillows, they told her the news: the old bridge was impassable now, they said, the water was so deep, they would have to go to their homes along the narrow muddy lanes. Night fell, and the last shift came in, puffing and panting after cycling or walking against the driving rain.

As Hetty tired again, she became more agitated. "Where is my river?" she kept asking, turning restlessly towards the window. The nurses thought she must be afraid, and brought her a tablet, and at last her eyes closed. The nursing home became silent.

And as Hetty slept, far away in the still, black night the river raced with renewed strength. Upstream more tributaries had formed torrents adding to the swollen floods. With a voice like an engine, the Wye swirled the old bridge aside in great chunks of wood and stone, hurtled onwards towards the city, and there it ran amok. The main force of water poured on, carrying trees and other debris with it, but near "River View" the overflow crept, stealthily and silently over the water meadows, slowly and inexorably approaching the house, lapping at the stone steps. The inmates slept deeply, Hetty stirred and murmured, and in the day room the nurses chatted and watched television. At about 3am someone went downstairs to make tea, and opened the back door. Six inches and rising!

The alarm was raised, the Fire Brigade arrived. The excited nurses joked. "Like being on the Ark!" some said. "Send out the budgie to look for land!" another giggled. The cellars were pumped out, rows of sandbags heaved into position, order restored. Work had started to divert the water, the rain stopped and the floods were already subsiding.

The immediate danger over, the nurses did their rounds. When they reached Hetty, however, she was far away. They saw her smiling, lying peacefully... What they could not know was that her beloved river had come to her after all, to bear her back to her happiest days.

Annie Says

Annie doesn't get on with the man next door. "With men like him about," she told me, "it's no wonder this country's on its feet."

If Wishes Were...

"Hi!" It said. "Yes?" I said

"I'll grant you three wishes. You can have anything."

"Why?" I said cynically. "Any purchase necessary?"

"Just get on with it or I'll change my mind" It said.

"I'm busy" I said. "Don't push me" It said.

I was by the window, watching my neighbour Mrs Bailey coming out of her house. Quite a picture: large surgical collar, one arm in a sling, dark glasses, white stick — had I seen that white stick before? She began to inch her way down her path and I dodged behind the curtains.

"Oh no!" I said. "She's coming over here again to share her problems. I've so much to do."

"Three wishes," it said sourly. "You won the competition."

"Of course I didn't" I said sharply.

"Come on" It said "Just hurry up." I wasn't listening.

"There's Mrs Bailey" I said. "Yesterday she had crutches. The day before she had a steel cage round her head. Last week she came in an electric wheelchair. An eye patch. Calipers. Why me? I wish someone would do something about her."

"Well..." It said.

"Hey" I said. "Just look at Mrs Bailey! She's running down the road, laughing, jumping! She's thrown her collar into one garden and her stick in another! She's shouting and dancing and shaking people's hands!" I was grinning too — then suddenly "Oh my stars, she's coming back this way — and fast — I bet she's coming to tell me what's happened — now look what you've done!" I said bitterly.

"Second" It said stiffly.

"Second!" I said. "Couldn't be worse!"

"It's a bit cold" It suggested. "Do you like sunshine?"

"No I snapped. "Leave this to me. You offered, I didn't ask...

"You'll have to be quick" It said, sounding hurt.

"Alright" I said "I'll have a cat."

"You'll have a what?" It said. "You hate cats!"

"I know" I said. "You said I could choose. If you're going to quibble..."

"Why a cat?" It persisted.

"Well" I said "Mrs Bailey hates cats too."

A large tabby appeared at the kitchen door. Long thin legs with cruel claws. Bony head to rub against your legs. Cold calculating eyes. I gulped and turned pale. It took a step towards me. Mrs Bailey was leaping up my path.

"I knew you wouldn't like it!" It said. "Third?"

Mrs Bailey opened the letter box and looked in.

The cat's tail twitched. She didn't see it but I did.

"Get rid of it!" I cried.

"What!" It was furious.

"The cat goes!" I yelled. "Get rid of the cat!"

The tabby disappeared, looking surprised.

Mrs Bailey put her mouth to the letter-box and started to sing "Oh what a beautiful morning" ringing the bell at the same time with her foot.

"Well there's your three wishes" It said.

"Just go" I said. "I should have checked your identification before I let you in."

"You've been wasting my time" It said. "You've missed your chance. I'm really disappointed in you. You could have saved the world."